1 The Statue Walks at Night

Joan Lowery Nixon

Illustrated by Kathleen Collins Howell

New York

With love to Brian and Sean Quinlan,
my inspiration for the Casebusters

—J.L.N.

Text copyright © 1995 by Joan Lowery Nixon.
Illustrations copyright © 1995 by Disney Press.
All rights reserved.
No part of this book may be used or reproduced in any manner whatsoever
without written permission from the publisher.
Printed in the United States of America.
For information address Disney Press, 114 Fifth Avenue,
New York, New York 10011.

FIRST EDITION
1 3 5 7 9 10 8 6 4 2

Library of Congress Catalog Card Number: 94-71791
ISBN: 0-7868-3046-8 / 0-7868-4018-8 (pbk.)

CHAPTER ONE

Sean Quinn shoved his chair back from the dinner table.

"I'm not going to take a bath tonight," he announced to his family. "Sam Miyako said that alligators can travel thousands of miles through sewers, from city to city, and suddenly pop up in your bathtub."

Mrs. Quinn sighed. "Sam Miyako strikes again," she said.

Brian, Sean's thirteen-year-old brother, narrowed his eyes. "And if they're big enough," he said teasingly, "they could crawl out of the bathtub and into your bedroom."

"The story's not true," Mr. Quinn

explained to Sean. "In the first place, sewers are not connected from one city to another." As his father explained to Sean about city regulations and sewer systems, Sean began to fidget.

"But Sam Miyako says it's true," Sean insisted.

Mrs. Quinn gave Brian a stern look. "I like Sam," she told Brian. "And I'm glad he's your best friend. But he has got to stop trying to scare the younger children."

"I'm not so young, Mom," Sean insisted, and sat up taller. "I'm nine."

"Isn't that too old to believe everything Sam Miyako tells you?" Mr. Quinn asked Sean.

Sean shrugged. "I guess so."

"I'll make you a promise," Mrs. Quinn said. "If an alligator does show up in the bathtub, you can keep him for a pet."

Sean thought for a moment. The idea of having an alligator in his bathtub was scary, but it was fun thinking about having one as a pet. No one else in his class would have an alligator as a pet, Sean thought.

Not even Miss Know-It-All, Debbie Jean Parker.

Suddenly an alligator in the bathtub didn't seem so scary.

"Thanks, Mom," Sean said, grinning.

The doorbell rang as Brian and Sean finished clearing the table, and Mrs. Quinn got up to answer it. In a few minutes Mrs. Maggie Gomez, the curator of the Redoaks County Museum, followed Mrs. Quinn into the kitchen.

"John," Mrs. Gomez said. "Thank goodness you're home."

Mr. Quinn stood. "Maggie, you know our boys, Brian and Sean," he said.

"Of course," Mrs. Gomez answered, and smiled. "John," she said, turning back to Mr. Quinn, "something terrible has happened at the museum. I want to hire you as a private investigator."

"We'll talk in the den, where it's more comfortable," Mr. Quinn said. He turned to Brian and Sean. "Suppose you boys say good night."

Brian and Sean said good night, then

started up the stairs. But halfway up, Brian stopped.

"'*Suppose* you go upstairs,'" he whispered to Sean, "isn't the same as 'You *have* to go upstairs,' is it?"

"No," said Sean, catching on. "And 'Something terrible at the museum' sounds like an interesting case for a pair of private investigators!"

"Like us," Brian and Sean said together.

Growing up with a father who was a professional private investigator, Brian and Sean had had many opportunities to help him on his cases. It began because Mr. Quinn liked to "talk out a case" with himself. Talking out loud, he said, helped him think. Brian and Sean liked listening to their father. Sometimes he would stop talking and ask them what they thought about a case.

Brian and Sean especially liked that their father didn't consider their questions or comments silly just because they were kids. He said that being a kid could actually be an advantage to an investigator. A kid could look at something with a different perspective than an adult, he said. And being able to look at evidence from different angles was often the key to cracking a case.

After a while, Mr. Quinn began to treat Brian and Sean almost as if they were his assistants. Their help had paid off, too. In one recent case, for instance, Brian and Sean had helped their father prove that it wasn't a ghost who was haunting the Pine Tree Inn. In another case, Brian and Sean had uncovered evidence that called into question the authenticity of a mysterious photograph of "Bigfoot."

From where they sat on the stairs, Brian and Sean could hear the urgency in Mrs. Gomez's voice.

"The Redoaks County Museum has what is claimed to be a foolproof security system," she explained, "but in spite of all our precautions, two extremely valuable sketches by Leonardo da Vinci are missing."

"Missing?" said Mr. Quinn. "Do you mean stolen?"

Mrs. Gomez sighed. "Yes."

"I'm familiar with the galleries in your museum, Maggie, but I don't remember any da Vinci sketches," Mr. Quinn said.

"The sketches don't belong to the museum," Mrs. Gomez said. "That's what makes the theft even worse. They're from a traveling exhibit on loan from the Metropolitan Museum of Art in New York. We've heavily advertised the exhibit, and it's scheduled to go on display in just one week. If the sketches aren't found by then . . ." Her voice broke as she cried, "I'm responsible for the safety of that collection, John! What am I going to do?"

"Maggie," Mr. Quinn said in his calm, professional private investigator's voice. "Call the police about the theft. They'll be able to search the museum. Also, they'll be able to get warrants to search your employees' homes. That's something that as a private investigator I don't have the legal right to do."

"I *have* called the police," Mrs. Gomez told him. "That's the first thing I did. I also called our insurance company. I was told by the manager of their theft division that ordinarily they would bring in one of their own investigators immediately. But sometimes they prefer to hire private investigators, especially in cases that need to be solved quickly—like this one. He gave me *your* name, John. He knew you'd not only be efficient but would keep the situation as quiet as possible."

"Then let's start with a few questions," Mr. Quinn said.

Brian imagined that his father had pulled out the notebook and pen he always carried with him. A notepad and a pen, his father had explained many times before, are a private investigator's most important tools. Brian, who planned to someday become a private investigator, too, pulled his own notebook and pen from a pocket in his jeans.

"Tell me the story from the beginning," Mr. Quinn urged, "noting exactly when you discovered that the sketches were missing."

"The cartons arrived three days ago," Mrs. Gomez said, "on Friday afternoon. My staff and I looked through them, checked the list, and everything was included. So I shelved the cartons in a special locked cabinet inside our large storeroom."

"Is the storeroom kept locked?" Mr. Quinn asked.

"No. Not during working hours. That would be inconvenient. And it's never been necessary," she said, "until now. I thought the exhibit material was safe, but this evening, when I took out the cartons to decide how to arrange the pieces in the exhibit, I discovered that two da Vinci sketches had been removed from their frames."

"Was the cabinet broken into?" Mr. Quinn asked.

"No."

Mr. Quinn looked up from his notepad. "Then whoever stole the art must have used a key."

Mrs. Gomez nodded. "My key, I'm afraid."

Mr. Quinn frowned. "How can you be so sure?" he asked.

Mrs. Gomez was embarrassed. "It's no secret that I keep the key in my top desk drawer," she said. "I guess it's not the safest place I could have thought of, but visitors aren't allowed back in the offices." She sighed. "After the theft I noticed that the key was not in its customary place in my drawer. Someone obviously had removed the key, then put it back. It's terrible to think that the thief is probably someone on my staff."

"Do all the employees know about the theft?" Mr. Quinn asked.

"The museum's security guard was there when the police arrived," Mrs. Gomez answered. "I telephoned my assistant, James Vanstedder. The other employees will be told tomorrow morning."

Mrs. Gomez took out a piece of paper from her briefcase and unfolded it on the table. "Here's a floor plan of the museum," she said. "You can see that the offices are together, in the back."

Mr. Quinn asked, "Where's your key to the cabinet now?"

"Here, with me, so that I won't have to worry about losing anything else in the collection."

"I assume all the items in the exhibit are valuable?"

"Oh yes," Mrs. Gomez said. "Some lovely, small Monet paintings, a Rembrandt drawing, and many other beautiful pieces. Everything in the collection is extremely valuable."

"Then I suggest that first thing tomorrow you call a locksmith to change the lock on the cabinet in which the exhibit pieces are stored. The thief could return. Most likely, he—or she—has already made a duplicate key."

Mrs. Gomez gasped.

Mr. Quinn asked, "How small were the sketches? Could they have been slipped into someone's pocket?"

"Not likely," Mrs. Gomez said. "One is

about sixteen inches by eighteen inches. The other is a little larger. Folding would ruin them. Because the thief carefully removed the sketches from their frames, I'm guessing that he'd know better than to fold them."

"But the sketches could be rolled, couldn't they?" Mr. Quinn asked. "And possibly carried out inside someone's clothing?"

Mrs. Gomez thought for a moment. "They *could* be tightly rolled, I suppose. But I should think it would be difficult to carry them out in that manner. Visitors to the museum are required to check all bags and jackets at the entrance. And our security guard is authorized to search bags and clothing as well. The sketches would be easy to detect, say, inside a sleeve or jacket. They would have made a suspicious bulge."

"Something about the theft puzzles me," Mr. Quinn said. "The missing sketches are from a famous artist. How could the thief expect to sell them without getting caught? Everyone he tried to sell them to would know the sketches belonged in a museum.

Also, why would he take just the two pieces when everything in the collection is valuable?"

"You'd be surprised at the large market for stolen art," Mrs. Gomez said sadly. "There are wealthy art collectors all over the world who knowingly buy stolen pieces and keep them in their own private collections, where they can't be discovered. Often, certain items are stolen on order."

"On order?" asked Mr. Quinn.

"Yes," said Mrs. Gomez. She explained, "It's not unheard-of that a wealthy art patron who has had his or her eye on a specific work of art might actually hire thieves to steal it. I suspect that is what happened with the two da Vinci sketches."

"That would explain why only two pieces were stolen," Mr. Quinn said. "Maggie, tell me about your employees."

Mrs. Gomez sighed. "The theft must have taken place on either Saturday or Sunday. I can tell you where all the employees were at the time."

As she spoke, Brian took notes as fast as

he could. When she finished, he sighed with relief and rubbed his hand.

Mr. Quinn resumed questioning Mrs. Gomez. "Is there a possibility that the sketches haven't been removed from the museum yet?"

Mrs. Gomez looked confused. "Why would a thief hide the sketches *in* the museum?"

"It occurred to me," Mr. Quinn explained, "that whoever took the sketches might have only temporarily hidden them."

"The police already searched through the employees' desks," Mrs. Gomez said, "and through all the file cabinets and in the storeroom, with no luck. They even searched behind the larger paintings hanging in the galleries. I can't imagine where the art could be hidden."

Mr. Quinn nodded. "I'll need a complete list of the items in the collection, including a full description of each work of art and its estimated value," Mr. Quinn said. "Also, I'll need a list of all your employees and their personnel files."

Brian and Sean exchanged a knowing look. As usual, their father was going to begin his investigation with a computer search. The object of the search was to discover as much as he could about the museum employees. Then the information would be used to create profiles of possible suspects.

Computers were a useful tool, but as Brian and Sean knew, a computer search took time. And time was something they didn't have a lot of.

"Sean!" Brian whispered later, after his father had concluded his interview with Mrs. Gomez. "Come on upstairs. Quick! We need to talk."

CHAPTER TWO

Both boys were seated cross-legged on Brian's bed, facing each other. Brian flipped open his notebook.

"Listen again to what Mrs. Gomez said about her employees and see if anything sounds strange to you," he said. He began to read aloud from his notes.

"Hilda Brown, Mrs. Gomez's secretary, has been away from the museum since Saturday afternoon, taking care of her elderly mother, who's ill. She'll return tomorrow—Tuesday."

"Nothing suspicious about that," Sean said. Brian agreed.

"Dave Brandon, the museum's newest

employee, had the weekend off. He went to San Francisco to talk to an art investor who is considering buying two paintings from a New York dealer and donating them to the museum."

"Bri," Sean said, "do you think Dave Brandon could really be trying to *sell* that dealer two sketches?"

"It's possible," Brian said, and continued reading.

"Charles Wang is head of the museum's financial department. When the theft occurred, he supposedly was at home with the flu. James Vanstedder, Mrs. Gomez's assistant, hurt his right leg while water-skiing Saturday."

"Didn't Mrs. Gomez say she telephoned him as soon as she discovered the theft this evening?" Sean asked.

"That's right," Brian said. "He came into work today, even though he hobbled around, leaning on a cane."

"Who's next?" Sean asked.

"Harvey Marshall," Brian said, "the elderly custodian. He was around the entire weekend, but Mrs. Gomez insists that she trusts him completely."

Brian flipped to the final entry in his notebook.

"Last on her list was George Potts, the security guard. Mrs. Gomez trusts him, too, because the only time George ever comes near the offices is when he walks his rounds each evening, making sure that everything is locked up securely and the alarms are in good order."

"Only two of the people on that list were in the museum the whole time," Sean said. "The custodian and the security guard."

Brian thought for a moment. "We have to go over there," he said.

"But Dad said he's going to check on the employees," Sean reminded him.

"I know that," Brian answered. "But that will take time. You and I can help Dad in the meantime by making a thorough search of the museum."

"You mean," Sean asked, "even the Egyptian room?"

Brian frowned. "C'mon, Sean," he said.

"Don't tell me you're still spooked about that dumb Anubis story."

"Heck no," Sean said. "I mean, not *really*."

On display in the Egyptian room was a mummy with its finger bones poking through the rotted wrappings. The display gave Sean the creeps. But even worse, watching over that mummy was a large bronze statue of the ancient Egyptian protector of mummies, the jackal-faced Anubis.

Sam Miyako had convinced Sean that everyone knew that the statue of Anubis *arose and walked at night!*

Sean had had nightmares about the statue ever since. Each time he dreamed that the statue came to life and walked slowly toward him. Sean always woke up yelling.

"All sorts of strange things happen in museums at night," Sam had told Sean.

"It's just a silly legend," Sean's father had explained. "The statue is made out of bronze. And bronze is an alloy of copper and tin—metals. Metals don't walk." He then had gone on to describe for Sean in tedious detail the unique chemical properties of bronze, none of which Sean could understand.

His mother had tried a less scientific but no less logical approach with Sean.

"The story doesn't make sense when you think about it," Mrs. Quinn had said. "No one's ever in the museum at night, which means that even if the statue tap-danced, no one would see it."

Sean had to admit that his mother was right. The story *didn't* make sense. Now, however, even thinking about Anubis made Sean shiver. He thought of the darkened museum, and Anubis with its gleaming eyes, and him alone in the museum!

Sean groaned. He had been excited by this new case. But *now* he was wondering if it would really be such fun after all.

CHAPTER THREE

The next day in class at Redoaks Elementary School, Sean couldn't keep his mind on what he was reading or on what his teacher, Mrs. Jackson, was saying. He was too excited thinking about the museum and trying to imagine where the thief might have hidden the da Vinci sketches. For some reason, sitting in class, Sean wasn't as scared by the Anubis story. He was even looking forward to going to the museum.

In history class that afternoon, Sean noticed that something black and lumpy was crawling slowly across his desk. He held his breath. It was a large, hairy tarantula!

"Aaaah!" screamed Sean.

Across the aisle Debbie Jean Parker giggled. Some of the other kids seated near Sean began to laugh, too.

"What's going on back there?" Mrs. Jackson asked.

"Sorry, Mrs. Jackson," Debbie Jean answered primly. "The tarantula I brought for my science report got loose. I guess it scared Sean." She grinned at Sean as she calmly reached over to his desk, picked up the tarantula, and placed it back inside a mesh-screened carrier.

Sean felt his face grow hot. "I wasn't scared of that dumb old tarantula," he insisted.

"You sure sounded scared," Debbie Jean snickered.

"Never mind," Mrs. Jackson said. "The tarantula took Sean by surprise, and he reacted the way any of us would have." Mrs. Jackson made a face. "Including me."

Sean liked Mrs. Jackson. Her smile made her black eyes sparkle, and she always knew the right things to say.

"Suppose we close our history books and let Debbie Jean give her science report now," Mrs. Jackson said. "We've got just enough time before class is dismissed."

In spite of being mad at Debbie Jean, Sean was fascinated by her report. At one point during her presentation he even stopped wishing that the tarantula would eat her notes and then munch on Debbie Jean for dessert. What she said about tarantulas was entertaining *and* interesting. And Sean knew that, as usual, she'd probably get an A.

Debbie Jean was smart. She could also tell good jokes and was a better pitcher than most of the kids on the fourth-grade baseball team, including Sean. But to him the sickening thing about Debbie Jean was that she always had to be right about everything. Just once, Sean wished Debbie Jean could be wrong about something.

Mrs. Jackson glanced at the clock, then made an announcement to the class.

"I'm pleased that all of you remembered to turn in your permission slips for our field trip to the museum tomorrow," she said.

The field trip! Sean realized that he had forgotten to tell Brian about his class's upcoming trip to the museum! He'd have another chance to look around the museum for clues without anyone on the museum staff becoming suspicious. But what kind of clues? Sean wondered.

"The museum's curator will be telling us the stories behind some of the paintings in their exhibit of American primitive art," said Mrs. Jackson, "so be sure to bring notebooks and pencils. After the trip I'll expect each of you to write a report about what you saw and learned."

A few kids groaned, but the bell rang and Mrs. Jackson dismissed the class for the day.

Sean grabbed his books, stuffed them into his backpack, and ran all the way to the museum, where Brian was waiting for him.

"I have a plan," Brian said as soon as Sean came up the steps.

Sean smiled. Brian always came up with some kind of a plan.

"We're going to start with a search of the first exhibit room on the right—the early weapons room. We'll check out as many of the exhibit rooms as we can. If we keep our eyes open, maybe we'll see something that might look suspicious, or strange, or out of place."

"But Mrs. Gomez said the police already searched the museum last night," Sean said.

"That's true," Brian said. "But we might discover something the police missed."

Brian and Sean entered the museum.

"Look," whispered Sean. "The museum guard is watching us. Do you think he knows what we're doing?"

"Don't worry about him," Brian said. "The minute grown-ups see kids hanging around, they start worrying that they're going to break stuff or make noise. It'll never occur to the guard that we're investigating a crime."

Sean froze, however, when he saw the

guard heading toward them.

"Uh-oh," he whispered to Brian.

"You'll have to check those backpacks and jackets, boys," the guard said. Then he walked away.

Brian looked at Sean. "See, I told you."

Brian and Sean checked their bags and jackets and entered the large main room of the museum, where the special exhibits were displayed.

A series of movable screens were arranged in a square in the center of the room and were hung with paintings belonging to the exhibit of American primitive art. Only a few people were viewing the exhibit. At this late afternoon hour there weren't many museum visitors.

On a far wall Brian saw a poster that announced the dates of the coming exhibit from the Metropolitan Museum of Art.

"C'mon," Brian said, and he and Sean entered the early weapons room, in which were displayed weapons dating back to the Civil War and the frontier days of the American West.

Brian immediately began examining the undersides of the glass display cases, checking to see if the stolen sketches could be hidden either underneath or inside them.

"Hey, come here, Bri!" Sean called out. "Look at this cane that's in two pieces. The handle has a short sword that can be hidden inside the cane."

Sean pressed his face closer to the glass.

"Neat," he said. He turned to Brian. "Someone could just pull on the carved top of the cane and *zap!* Out comes the sword! Wow! If I had a sword like this one, I'd go like *wham* and *zap* and *whoosh!*"

"We're supposed to be looking for hiding places," Brian said. "Remember?"

But Sean's attention was focused on the sword. He dashed between the cases, fighting with an imaginary enemy.

"Cut it out," Brian warned him. "You're making so much racket the guard will be in here to see what you're doing."

"He can't come in here because he'd have to leave his post," Sean said.

Suddenly a deep voice spoke from behind them.

"Hey, you kids!" the guard said sternly. "Keep it down."

"I thought he wasn't supposed to leave his post," Sean whispered to Brian after the guard walked away.

"The museum's not that large," Brian said. "The guard's able to keep an eye on everything." Brian scowled at Sean. "So stop acting up!" Sometimes, Brian was thinking, younger brothers can be such a pain.

The boys began searching the room, but with no luck.

"We might as well move on to the California history room," Brian said finally. "We didn't find what we were looking for in here."

As they entered the main gallery, Sean spotted some illustrated pamphlets on a table. He picked one up and read through it. It was about the pieces in the American primitive art collection. Sean put the pamphlet down. He'd find out more than he wanted to know about all that stuff tomorrow during the field trip. Then he had an idea. A big grin came over his face.

He folded the pamphlet and stuck it in the pocket of his jeans. If all went well, he told himself, he had a plan that would drive Debbie Jean Parker crazy.

Brian had already finished exploring the California history room by the time Sean caught up to him.

"I can't find any hiding places in here," Brian told Sean. "We'll try the Egyptian room next."

Sean froze. The Egyptian room! He had almost forgotten about it.

"Let's not," Sean said, hesitating. But he followed Brian anyway. At the entrance to the Egyptian room, his gaze was drawn across the room to the jackal-faced statue of Anubis that loomed over the glass case in which the mummy lay entombed. Sean shivered with fright. What if Sam really *was* right? What if the legend of Anubis wasn't just a silly story?

"Bri, why don't we look through the art

galleries on the other side of the museum?" Sean suggested.

"Because we're here and not there," Brian insisted impatiently.

No other visitors were in the Egyptian room, and the few people who had been viewing the exhibit in the main room had drifted off to the art galleries.

Sean inched closer to Brian.

"This is the same as the other two rooms we were in," he whispered. "There's nothing but cases full of things and pictures of Egyptian tombs and stuff hanging on the walls. No place to hide anything. Let's get out of here."

But Brian was staring at the statue of Anubis. "Shhh," he said. "Did you hear anything?"

"Don't do that, Bri!" whined Sean. He was about to punch his brother's arm but stopped as he saw a look of alarm creep across Brian's face.

"Shhh!" Brian said. A distinct scraping sound was coming from the statue. "It moved," Brian whispered.

The scraping grew louder, and suddenly the statue slowly turned so that it was looking right at them!

"Look out!" Sean yelled. "It's coming after us!"

CHAPTER FOUR

A face popped up at the side of the statue.

"Hello, boys," the man said. He was dressed in gray overalls and carried a large rag in his front pocket.

He must be the custodian, Harvey Marshall, Brian thought. Brian walked up to him and smiled.

"What are you doing, sir?" he asked. He tried to appear interested. Brian had learned from his investigations that adults usually weren't much interested in what kids had to say or what they thought about anything, but they could easily be coaxed into talking about themselves. In doing so, sometimes they would accidentally let slip an important bit of information.

Harvey Marshall smiled back and wiped the rag across his sweaty forehead.

"It's the darndest thing," he said, peering at the statue.

"What?" asked Brian.

Harvey Marshall shook his head. "I can't figure it out, but somehow this statue is not in the same spot it was yesterday."

Sean suddenly pricked up his ears.

"You mean it *moved*?" he asked Mr. Marshall. His eyes had grown wide with alarm.

"Doesn't seem likely, does it?" Mr. Marshall said. Then he nodded his head. "But I'm sure of it. The statue moved." He pointed to the floor. "See for yourself."

Brian knelt down and examined the tiles next to the base of the statue. They were slightly darker and less worn than the others.

"He's right," Brian told Sean excitedly.

Brian stood up. "I wonder how it could have moved," he said.

Sean already had a pretty good idea. He

was thinking about Sam Miyako and the legend of Anubis.

Just then Brian tapped lightly on the side of the statue.

"Hey!" said Mr. Marshall suddenly to Brian. "That's a work of art. Don't go banging on it."

"Sorry," said Brian. He turned to Sean. "The statue's too light to be solid," he whispered. "It must be hollow."

"So?" said Sean.

Brian smiled and turned back to Mr. Marshall. "Is there a way of getting into the statue?" he asked.

"Don't ask me," Mr. Marshall said.

"No secret panels?" Sean asked.

Mr. Marshall chuckled. "If you're thinking of hidden treasure from the tombs, then you've been watching too many adventure movies."

"Where'd the statue come from?" Sean asked.

"I don't know," Mr. Marshall answered. "It's been here as long as I have."

Sean cleared his throat twice before he

could ask, "Somebody told me that the statue walks at night. Is that true?"

"So I've heard," Mr. Marshall said.

Sean gave a start and moved closer to Brian. "You mean the story is true?"

"Of course the story isn't true," said Brian, scoffing. "Isn't that right?" he asked Mr. Marshall.

"*I've* never seen the statue walk, if that's what you're asking," he answered. "And I'm not going to. You'll never catch me here in the museum at night."

Mr. Marshall shoved the statue back into place, then wiped it clean with his rag.

"Don't that beat all?" he murmured suddenly, looking at the rag in his hand.

"What?" Brian asked.

"This stain," Mr. Marshall said. "It looks like blood, but it couldn't be."

Brian immediately dropped to his knees and carefully studied the base of the statue.

"Look," Brian said. "I must have missed it before, but there's another small stain, here on the metal near the wood stand." He jumped to his feet. "Mr. Marshall, let's

see if we can lift the statue off the stand."

Mr. Marshall shook his head. "No thanks."

"But what if this *is* blood?" Brian asked.

"It isn't any of my concern if it is or if it isn't. My job is only to keep it clean. Anyway, I never should have said it looked like blood and got you kids all riled up. More than likely, that stain is just polish. Now why don't you kids run along and let me get back to work."

Brian was about to ask some more questions when Sean took him by the arm.

"Bri," said Sean as he led his brother toward the exit, "I really want to see the Asian art!"

"In a minute," Brian said.

"No, Brian. Right now!"

"What's the matter with you?" Brian asked once they were out of earshot of the Egyptian room. "You know how Dad works. Private investigators are supposed to stay cool, not jump around yelling about wanting to see Asian art."

"Oh yeah?" countered Sean. "I wasn't

jumping, and I wasn't yelling. I just wanted to get out of that room!"

Sean took a big breath. "Bri," he said, "what if that really was blood on the statue? Maybe the statue does walk at night. The blood we found might be from its latest victim!"

"If you'll be quiet a second, I'll tell you what I think." Brian lowered his voice. "The statue could be the thief's hiding place."

"Are you sure?" Sean asked.

"No, I'm not," Brian said. "But it makes sense. The statue is hollow. If the thief expected Mrs. Gomez to call the police as soon as she discovered the theft of the sketches, he'd also expect that the employees' houses would be searched, too. The statue is fastened to the stand with only four screws that wouldn't be hard to remove. It's a really good place to hide the art."

"Do you think the stolen sketches could be in the statue now?"

"I don't know."

"Should we tell Dad?" asked Sean.

Brian frowned as he thought. "If we do, he might find the sketches, but he wouldn't find out who put them there. If we're lucky, *we* might discover the thief."

"How?" Sean asked.

"The metal at the bottom of the statue has some rough edges. My guess is that the thief cut his hand on them. That would explain the blood."

"That means the thief's probably going around with a bandage on his hand," Sean said. He smiled. "This is so easy. All we need to do is check all the suspects' hands."

"I don't think it's going to be that easy," Brian told him. "We may not get a chance to see their hands. Mr. Marshall is a suspect. Did you see his hands?"

"No, because he was wearing work gloves."

At that moment Mr. Marshall came out of the Egyptian room and headed for the storeroom. As he walked he tugged off his gloves.

"Look," Sean said. "No bandage."

"Right," said Brian.

"Can we check some of the other employees to see if they have bandages on their hands?" Sean asked.

"Sure," Brian said, "but let's see if we can get a set of fingerprints from the statue first. If Dad gets prints from the employees, we might find a set that matches."

Back inside the Egyptian room, Sean pulled a small bottle of finely ground charcoal powder and a soft brush from his pocket. As part of his investigator's kit, Brian also carried a small flashlight, a pair of tweezers, and envelopes to collect evidence in. Sometimes he carried a tape recorder that was smaller than a wallet.

Brian carefully brushed the lower part of the statue with powder, then clicked on his flashlight. He ran the beam slowly over the powder.

"Darn," said Brian finally. "The thief must have wiped the statue clean. There aren't any fingerprints."

"How about trying a little higher?" Sean

asked. "I can see some fingerprints right here."

"Where we were holding it," Brian said. "Those prints are yours and mine."

"If the thief wiped away his prints, then why didn't he wipe away the blood?" Sean asked.

"He probably would have if he'd seen it," Brian said. "Sometimes you can get a cut that bleeds and not notice it for a while. That might be what happened."

"Now what?" Sean asked.

"Let's go to the business offices and see if we can get a look at the other suspects," Brian said.

"They don't let visitors in. Remember?" Sean said.

Brian tucked away his brush and the bottle of powder.

"We're friends of Mrs. Gomez's," Brian said. "We can drop by to say hello to her." He and Sean walked down the hallway and opened the door that led into the museum's business offices.

A thin, gray-haired woman, with silver-rimmed glasses resting halfway down her long nose, looked up from behind a reception desk and glared at them.

She must be Hilda Brown, Mrs. Gomez's secretary, Brian thought.

"Hi," he said. "We're Brian and Sean Quinn. We'd like to see Mrs. Gomez." Brian sneaked a quick glance around the office. There were doors to four offices. Three were closed.

"Children are not allowed back here," Ms. Brown said curtly. She pointed to the door. "Please leave. Immediately."

Sean let out a low whistle as he saw the bandage wrapped around the palm of Hilda Brown's right hand.

"Mrs. Gomez is a good friend of our parents'," Brian told her. "I think she'd want to see us."

"Mrs. Gomez is very busy," Ms. Brown said.

Sean nodded toward her bandage. "How'd you hurt your hand?" he asked.

"My cat," she said, looking sharply at Sean. "She nipped me."

"That's too bad," Sean said. Of course, he thought to himself, if *he* were Hilda Brown's cat, he might feel like biting her, too.

Just then a deep voice called out from behind the only open office door.

"Hilda, could you come in here and discuss these invoices?"

Ms. Brown rose from her chair, still scowling at Brian and Sean. "Stay right here until I get back," she snapped. "I'll decide then whether or not Mrs. Gomez will have time to see you."

As soon as Ms. Brown was out of sight, Brian and Sean tiptoed to the door that had Mrs. Gomez's name on it and silently opened it. Brian was about to say hello when he noticed that Mrs. Gomez was on the phone. She had her back turned to the door and didn't notice the boys enter.

"John!" she cried into the phone. "I've just discovered something horrible! The Monet paintings have also disappeared from the collection!"

Brian and Sean exchanged looks. The

"John" she was talking to was their dad. Their father must have asked when the paintings had been taken because Mrs. Gomez then said, "Sometime after I examined the collection yesterday and before the locksmith changed the lock on the storage cabinet this morning."

Suddenly Sean nudged Brian and pointed. Mrs. Gomez was waving her left hand as she spoke. There was a gauze bandage across her palm!

CHAPTER FIVE

Brian and Sean stepped back, and Brian quietly closed the door to Mrs. Gomez's office.

"Maybe Mrs. Gomez took the art," Sean said to Brian. "Then she hired Dad to investigate, thinking that nobody'd suspect the person who hired the investigator."

Brian nodded slowly. "It's possible."

Ms. Brown suddenly appeared behind them. "Boys," she barked, "I told you to wait right where you were!"

Ms. Brown's lips pursed as though she'd just swallowed a caterpillar. "Mrs. Gomez will see you now," she announced. "Don't keep her waiting."

Under Ms. Brown's watchful eye, Brian and Sean hurried into Mrs. Gomez's office.

Mrs. Gomez smiled when they came in, but Brian noticed that she seemed flustered.

"We just dropped by to say hello," Brian said.

"So, we'll be going now," Sean added. "Good-bye."

Brian clamped a hand on Sean's shoulder. "You don't have a cafeteria in the museum," Brian said.

"Huh?" Sean stared at Brian.

"This museum isn't large enough to warrant a cafeteria," Mrs. Gomez said. She opened a side drawer of her desk. "If you're hungry, I have an apple and some cheese crackers in here."

"No thanks," Brian said. "I'm not hungry. I was just wondering how the people who work in the museum eat lunch. I guess they brown-bag it."

Mrs. Gomez laughed. "That's a strange thing to wonder about."

Brian smiled back. "I was just curious."

"Well, to satisfy your curiosity," she explained, "with the exception of our security guard, George Potts, most of the museum employees leave the museum during lunchtime. George and Harvey bring their lunch and stay during the day without leaving. Harvey takes George's place as guard while George is on his breaks. The rest of us usually eat at nearby restaurants. Hilda's apartment isn't far from here, so she goes home at lunchtime to feed her cat."

Just then there was a knock on the office door. It was flung open a second later by a tall, tanned, elegantly dressed man who clumped into the room, leaning on a cane. He smiled at the boys.

"Sorry, Maggie," he said. "I didn't know you were busy."

"Come in, James," Mrs. Gomez said. "I'd like you to meet my friends, Brian and Sean. Boys," she said, "this is Mr. James Vanstedder, the museum's assistant curator."

Mr. Vanstedder winced as he shifted his cane from his right hand to his left so he

could shake hands. Brian and Sean both zeroed in on Mr. Vanstedder's left hand, which was wrapped in a thick gauze bandage.

What is with the people in this museum? Sean wondered. *Do they all have bandaged hands?*

Mr. Vanstedder gave an embarrassed shrug. "I guess I must look pretty battered," he said. "I was water-skiing and got all tangled up in my skis, and, well . . . this is what happened."

"Poor James," Mrs. Gomez said. "What did the doctor say?"

"The doctor?" he repeated.

"When you saw him this afternoon," Mrs. Gomez said.

"Oh," he said quickly. "Of course. The doctor. He just prodded and poked my leg and changed the bandages," Mr. Vanstedder explained. "He said I should be fine by this time next week."

Mr. Vanstedder looked at his watch and smiled apologetically at Brian and Sean. "I hope I'm not rushing your guests, Maggie, but you promised that at four-thirty we could discuss how we're going to exhibit the Metropolitan collection. Time's running out."

"Yes, it is." Suddenly Mrs. Gomez looked frantic.

Brian and Sean thanked Mrs. Gomez for her time and said a quick good-bye.

"By the way," Sean asked Mrs. Gomez on his way out. "How did you hurt your hand?"

She looked down at her hand as if she were surprised to see the bandage. "I cut it on some metal staples that fastened one of the museum's cartons," she answered. "Why?"

Sean shook his head. "No reason. See you later."

"Where to now?" Sean asked Brian outside the museum offices.

"First the lecture hall," Brian said, "then the art galleries."

But after a thorough search of those rooms, the boys hadn't found anyplace where they thought the stolen sketches might be hidden.

"Let's go home," Brian told Sean finally. "We've got to talk, and I'll write up my notes on what we've seen and heard." Brian pulled out their claim check and headed for the counter where they'd left their backpacks and jackets.

As they passed under the watchful gaze of George Potts, Brian suddenly stopped. "Sir," he said, "I'm very much interested in museum security. Will you let me ask you a few questions?"

"You kids," Mr. Potts grumbled good-naturedly. "Go ahead. Ask away."

"Thanks," Brian said. Obviously, Brian thought, Mr. Potts assumed he and Sean were just another couple of kids with a dumb school project.

"I know you don't allow visitors to carry things—even coats—into or out of the museum," Brian said. "But how about the people who work here? If they leave with briefcases or boxes, do you trust them, or do you check the contents?"

"It's not up to me to trust anybody," Mr. Potts explained. "I just go by the rules. And according to the rules, every container of any kind taken out of the museum has to be examined. No exceptions."

"What about when Mr. Marshall takes your place?" Brian asked.

"He follows the rules, exactly as I do."

"Do the museum employees ever go in or out of the museum by the back doors?"

"Never," Mr. Potts said. "Those doors are unlocked during the day but are used only in emergencies. If anyone tries to open them, locked or unlocked, they set off the alarm system."

"Who controls the alarm system?"

Mr. Potts looked pleased with himself. "I do," he announced.

"But what if an employee stayed after you'd gone home?" Brian was thinking about the burglar alarm system they had at home. "He could turn off the alarm and reset it, couldn't he?"

"Not in my museum he couldn't!" Mr. Potts answered. "The curator and I are the only ones who know the combination."

Brian smiled, thanked Mr. Potts, and then he and Sean left the museum. Outside, Sean reminded Brian about his class field trip.

"Good," Brian told him. "I know exactly what you'll need to do."

CHAPTER SIX

Brian and Sean arrived home before their parents did. Through the windows in the garage door they could see that the garage was empty. Mrs. Quinn usually made it home by five o'clock from her job as a graphic artist at a small advertising agency in town. But Mr. Quinn was just as likely to show up early as late. His hours varied with the work he had to do on each case.

As the boys let themselves into the kitchen, the fax machine in their father's office rang once and beeped.

"Maybe we should see what the message is," Sean said.

"It's Dad's business, not ours," Brian told him.

"Unless Mom and Dad have been kidnapped by foreign spies," Sean suggested, "and are being held on a submarine until we come through with the ransom money. How are we going to know if we don't look?"

"You think someone's faxing Dad information he asked for that has to do with the museum thefts?"

Sean grinned. "It makes more sense than the kidnapping, doesn't it?"

The fax machine beeped again, signaling an end to the message.

"I guess it wouldn't hurt to look," Brian said.

Brian and Sean raced each other into their father's office and read the fax.

Sean frowned. "This says that Harvey Marshall was arrested and convicted on a charge of shoplifting when he was eighteen," Sean said. "But he's an old man now," he said. "What he did way back then shouldn't matter."

TUESDAY

"Police records don't go away," Brian said. Just then he discovered a legal-size sheet of paper lying on top of a folder on his father's desk. It was labeled "Redoaks County Museum." It was their father's notes on the case.

"Sean," he said, eyeing the sheet of paper. "It's not exactly like we're snooping into Dad's things if we're helping him on the case, is it?"

"Dad will be glad we helped him," Sean answered. "At least, he ought to be."

Brian began reading his father's notes.

"Listen to this," he said. "Hilda Brown recently withdrew most of the money from her savings account. She's been paying for nursing home care for her mother."

"She could probably get all the money she'd need if she sold the stolen art," Sean said.

"Dave Brandon borrowed more than twenty thousand dollars to pay his college expenses," Brian said, "and hasn't begun paying it back."

"So he needs money, too," Sean said.

"Except Mr. Brandon wasn't in Redoaks. He was in San Francisco when the sketches were stolen."

Sean thought about James Vanstedder, who had hobbled into Mrs. Gomez's office on his cane. "What did Dad write about Mr. Vanstedder?" he asked.

"Mr. Vanstedder owes a lot of money to half a dozen credit card companies. And he hasn't been able to pay the telephone company's charges for making a lot of calls to a number in Italy," Brian said. "He doesn't have a savings account, and there's less than two hundred dollars in his checking account."

"But remember," Sean said, "he got really banged up in that waterskiing accident. He couldn't be the thief. What did Dad write about Charles Wang, the accountant, and George Potts?"

"Nothing," Brian answered.

Sean sighed. "How could any of the museum people steal the sketches when they weren't even near the museum when the sketches disappeared?"

"They *claimed* they weren't there," Brian said. "But Ms. Brown could have left her mother with the nurses, returned to the museum, and gone back to the nursing home at any time during the weekend. Mr. Brandon could have returned much earlier from his business trip to San Francisco than he said he did. Knowing Dad, he's probably checking out their alibis."

"How?" Sean asked.

"By asking questions," Brian explained. Brian had been on enough cases with his dad to know the kinds of questions he asked.

"I bet Dad will ask the people at the nursing home if anyone saw Ms. Brown leave at any time," Brian said. "He'll probably check with the San Francisco hotel where Mr. Brandon stayed and find out what times he checked in and checked out. And he'll also ask about the phone calls he made to the New York art dealer." Brian nodded. "He might even talk to Mr. Vanstedder's doctor and to the people who run the water-ski rental about Mr.

Vanstedder's injury and find out more about those phone calls to Italy."

"OK," Sean said. He counted on his fingers. "If we include Mr. Marshall, then our list is back up to five suspects: Dave Brandon, James Vanstedder, Charles Wang, Harvey Marshall, and Hilda Brown."

"Six, if we count Mrs. Gomez," Brian said. "Remember, she had a bandage on her hand. And don't forget that we can't discount George Potts as a suspect, either."

"But he's the security guard," Sean said.

"Exactly," said Brian. "Who better to steal priceless works of art than the one person who controls the security system."

Sean let out a big sigh. "That's *seven* suspects."

The back door banged, and Mrs. Quinn called out, "Sean! Brian! I'm home!"

Brian and Sean hurried to the kitchen. Mrs. Quinn had already tossed her jacket on a chair and was rummaging through the refrigerator.

"I bought some barbecued chicken," she said, "and I've got some potatoes to bake in the microwave. Sound good?"

"Sounds great," Sean said, and hugged her.

"Who wants to set the table for me?" she asked.

Brian sprinted toward the door. "Sean will," he said. "I've got to get my history book back from Sam."

"You've got ten minutes," Mrs. Quinn said. "Don't stay next door talking and make me have to call you."

Sean followed Brian out to the backyard. "Dad's computer search turned up a lot of information," he said.

"But not enough," Brian answered.

"He'll come up with more."

Brian lowered his voice. "All that takes time, and time is what we haven't got. The exhibit is supposed to open in less than a week. I think we can help Dad if we—"

He stopped.

"If we what?" Sean asked.

"I have a plan," Brian said. "This is what I want you to do. Tomorrow, bring your camera to the museum and take pictures of everything you can. Try to get pictures of the employees we haven't met. On your way home stop off at the one-hour photo place to get the film developed."

"What will the pictures show us?"

"We won't know until we see them," Brian answered. "But we might discover something that will help us." He frowned. "The way things are going, we need all the help we can get!"

CHAPTER SEVEN

As Brian entered Sam Miyako's kitchen, something slapped him across the shoulders.

"Hiya!" yelled Sam's little brother, Charlie. He raised a long cardboard tube and aimed it at Brian. But Sam stepped in with a tube of his own, sending Charlie's tube flying.

"Mom's wrapping Charlie's birthday presents," Sam said as Charlie snatched up both tubes and ran from the room. "We were playing sword fight with the cardboard tubes inside the gift wrap."

"That reminds me," Brian said. "At the museum today I saw this weird sword that fits inside a hollow cane. It was supposed to be a hundred years old."

Sam put on a spooky accent. "Ze sword vas mebbe carried by a crazed vampire looking for victims caught in ze fog."

Brian grinned. "Vampires don't need swords. They have teeth."

"Eet vas an old, toothless vampire needing help."

"Bad guess."

"Eet vas a young vampire who kept hiz lunch money in ze cane and used ze sword to try to cut hiz school cafeteria food?"

"Funny, but hopeless," Brian said.

Sam shrugged. "Would your parents like to adopt me?" he suddenly asked.

"Don't tell me you're in trouble again," Brian said.

"Nobody in this house appreciates a good sense of humor," Sam said.

Brian groaned. "That means you scared your little brother again. Right?"

"I didn't think he'd get really scared. I mean, not enough to have nightmares. I just asked him if he knew that monsters live inside the walls of houses and ooze through the cracks at night and climb under beds to get warm."

"All I can say is, if you tell Sean that story, you won't get adopted, you won't get dinner, and you probably won't even get a friendly look from Mom or Dad."

"As I said, nobody appreciates a good sense of humor," Sam complained.

Brian laughed. "Hey, Sam," he said. "I need my history book back."

"No problem," Sam said. "I'll be right back." As Sam went to get the book, Brian wished Mrs. Gomez hadn't told his dad to keep the situation as quiet as possible. He would have liked to have told Sam about the museum thefts. Sam was his best friend and sometimes came up with very good ideas.

Later that evening, as Brian passed by Sean's bedroom, he poked his head inside and saw Sean sitting up in bed. He was reading the pamphlet he'd picked up at the museum and was laughing out loud to himself.

"You're weird," Brian said.

"Thank you," Sean said. "Debbie Jean Parker's going to think so, too."

"Don't forget your camera tomorrow," Brian said. "I'm eager to see if anything turns up in your photos."

The next morning, when Sean's class arrived at the museum for its tour, George Potts made an announcement.

"You may take pictures in the exhibit rooms," he explained, "but we don't allow flash pictures in the art galleries."

Debbie Jean saw the camera that was hanging around Sean's neck and smiled smugly. "All museums have this rule. The flash can damage paintings."

"Everybody knows that," Sean said, even though he hadn't. Just you wait, Debbie Jean Parker, he was thinking. Sean was so eager for the tour to begin, he could hardly hold still.

Mrs. Gomez greeted Mrs. Jackson and her class with a big smile, but Sean quickly noticed that Mrs. Gomez's eyelids drooped.

Sean figured that she hadn't had much sleep.

Mrs. Gomez led them to the special exhibit area in the main gallery. "The paintings you're about to see are called American primitive art," she said. "Do any of you know what is meant by American primitive art?"

Sean's hand shot up. His was the only one.

Mrs. Jackson looked surprised, then pleased.

"Sean?" Mrs. Gomez asked.

Sean stood as tall as he could and tried to look wise. "American primitive art," he began, "is a type of folk art made by artists without formal training. While it includes paintings by early American painters, such as Edward Hicks, and later primitive painters, such as Grandma Moses, American folk art also includes quilt making, sculpture of figureheads on boats, and other types of regional crafts."

"Very good, Sean!" Mrs. Gomez exclaimed. Mrs. Jackson beamed at him.

Sean tried not to burst out laughing when he saw Debbie Jean's openmouthed stare.

Debbie Jean struggled to regain control of herself. "Oh yeah?" she said. "Who's Sean calling Grandma Moses? I know she's not *his* grandma."

Everyone looked at Sean. Mrs. Gomez waited for him to say something. Sean searched his memory for what was written in that art pamphlet.

"Grandma Moses," he said, "was a farm wife who didn't start painting until she was in her seventies. Her real name was Anna Mary Robertson Moses."

Sean could tell from the smile on Mrs. Gomez's face that she had begun to catch on. That was OK with Sean. At least Debbie Jean hadn't. Her nose and cheeks were splotched an angry red, and she scowled at Sean as though she couldn't figure out what to do or say next.

"Suppose we take a look at one of Grandma Moses's paintings right now," Mrs. Gomez said. She winked at Sean.

"And after our tour of the exhibit, I hope you'll all take one of the pamphlets about the exhibit, which you'll find on a table near the front door."

Now that the fun with Debbie Jean was over, Sean didn't care if she found out that he'd memorized parts of the pamphlet. And Mrs. Jackson would be pleased that Sean had learned something on his own. Cheerfully he walked with his class through the exhibit, listening to what Mrs. Gomez said and making notes.

As soon as the tour was over, however, and the class was allowed to examine the rest of the museum on its own, Sean began taking pictures.

"What are you doing?" Debbie Jean asked him. "Why are you taking a picture of that crossbow? What are you doing in the weapons room, anyway, when we're supposed to be studying art?"

Sean tried to ignore her and aimed his camera at one of the cases.

Debbie Jean smoothed down her shirt and skirt and brushed back her hair with one hand as she stepped in front of the case. "I'll pose for you," she said. "Pictures are always more interesting with people in them."

Sean groaned. "Debbie Jean, get out of the way!" he grumbled. He moved around her, then took the picture.

When Sean tried taking pictures inside the early California history room and in the Egyptian room, however, Debbie Jean kept getting in his way. She even followed Sean when he walked through the door to the business offices.

"Why are you going in there?" she demanded. "You're not supposed to be in there. You'd better get out of there. You're going to get in trouble."

"Be quiet," Sean whispered. Inside the office, Sean was relieved to see that Hilda Brown wasn't at her desk. Probably her lunch hour, Sean thought. He snapped pictures as quickly as he could in every direction.

"Let's *go*," Debbie Jean whined.

"Not yet," Sean said. He carefully

opened the doors to the other offices.

The first two were empty. They belonged to Mr. Brandon and Mr. Wang. Mrs. Gomez's office was empty, too. Sean took pictures of everything.

Sean was feeling lucky until he opened the door to Mr. Vanstedder's office. Thinking it was empty, too, Sean calmly raised his camera and snapped a picture.

"What do you think you're doing?" boomed an angry voice.

Debbie Jean screamed and ran.

Sean stumbled sideways, accidentally knocking down Mr. Vanstedder's cane, which was leaning against the wall.

"I'm sorry, Mr. Vanstedder," Sean said as he picked up the cane. "I'm taking pictures of everything in the museum for a report I'm going to do."

Mr. Vanstedder, who was seated behind his desk, glanced from the cane to Sean. "You don't belong in the office area! Get out of here! Immediately!" he demanded.

Sean turned so fast that he collided with a tall young man, who grabbed him by his

shoulders. "What's this kid doing back here?" the man asked.

"Let him go, Dave," Mr. Vanstedder grumbled. "He belongs back with his class."

Dave Brandon, Sean thought.

He stared down at Sean. "I've been watching this kid take pictures of some pretty strange things," he said, "like the locks on the exhibit cabinets and the emergency exits. Do you know him, James?"

"I believe his name is Sean," Mr. Vanstedder said.

Sean spoke up. "It's Sean Quinn."

"Quinn?" Mr. Vanstedder said. "The private investigator Maggie hired is named Quinn."

"He's my dad," Sean said.

Both men reacted with surprise. Then Mr. Brandon quickly released Sean, and it was hard for Sean not to stare. The palm of Mr. Brandon's left hand was covered with a gauze bandage!

CHAPTER EIGHT

Debbie Jean was waiting for Sean just outside. "What took you so long?" she asked, but she didn't wait for an answer. "Mrs. Jackson told us to line up and get ready to go back to school."

"OK, OK," Sean said. They hurried back to the main gallery, where the class was already assembled in two neat rows.

"OK, class," Mrs. Jackson announced after she took roll call, "I want you to begin walking *in an orderly fashion* to the museum exit. The bus is waiting out front."

On the bus back to school, Debbie Jean let out a shriek. Sean chuckled.

"Mrs. Jackson!" Debbie Jean complained

loudly. "I just read the museum's art pamphlet! That's where Sean got all that information!"

Sean grinned and leaned back against the seat. True, he thought, he hadn't come across any clues yet that might solve the case of the stolen sketches, and he had been caught taking pictures in the wrong place. But all in all, it had been a very good day.

After school, Sean took his film to be developed and raced home without taking time to look at the photos. He found Brian in the kitchen munching his way through some fudge brownies. Sean shoved the package of photos into Brian's hands.

"Where's Mom?" Sean asked.

"She left a message on the answering machine. She's working overtime and is going to be late. She said to microwave the chicken noodle dinners in the freezer."

Brian began to look through the pictures, which gave Sean a chance to attack the brownies.

"Dad left a message, too," Brian said.

"He's going to be in a meeting."

As Sean stuffed half a brownie in his mouth, Brian held up one photo. "That's weird," he said. He pointed at something in the photo. "What's this blurred, lumpy thing off to the side?"

Sean leaned over Brian's shoulder and squinted at the photo. "Oh," he said, "that's Debbie Jean Parker's nose."

"What's it doing in the picture?"

"Don't blame me. I tried to keep it out."

Brian held up another photo. "Is this part of Debbie Jean, too?"

Sean studied the picture. "It might be her ear."

"Who's this guy?" Brian asked.

Sean picked up a photo he'd taken in the Egyptian room. Half a dozen kids from his class were bending over the exhibits. A man stood in the doorway watching them.

"That's Dave Brandon," Sean said. "I didn't notice him when I took the picture. Debbie Jean kept distracting me. You can see in the picture that his left hand is bandaged."

"I wonder why," Brian said.

"I didn't take the time to ask," Sean told him. He spread out some of the photos on the table.

"Look," Sean said around a mouthful of brownie. "There he is in the picture I took in the California history room. And there—he's standing in the doorway to the early weapons room."

"I wonder if he was following you," Brian said. "Maybe he was afraid you'd take flash photos of the art when you weren't supposed to."

Sean told Brian about how Mr. Brandon nabbed him in Mr. Vanstedder's office and how he had let go of Sean in a hurry when he found out who he was.

"It could be he wanted to make sure I didn't take pictures of something he wanted to hide," Sean said.

Brian looked through the other photos. "Hey! Great! You were able to get some pictures in the office area. Here's Hilda Brown's desk with some cartons and . . . What's this big brown thing?"

Sean sighed. "Debbie Jean's shoe."

Brian studied the rest of the pictures. "There's Mr. Vanstedder," he said. "And I suppose this thing in the corner is another part of your friend Debbie Jean."

"She's *not* my friend. She's something weird that was dumped here by hostile aliens from outer space." Sean pointed at the photo. "That's Mr. Vanstedder's cane," he said. "I accidentally knocked it down, and he got really mad at me."

Brian frowned. "Wait a minute," he said. "Mr. Vanstedder's seated behind his desk, but his cane's way across the room, near the door to his office. He needs the cane for support, so why would he prop it so far from his desk? How would he get to it?"

"Hop on one foot?" Sean suggested.

Brian's eyes lit up as he remembered the hollow cane with the sword in it and Sam's joke about a vampire keeping his lunch money in a hollow cane. "Was the cane heavy or light?" he asked Sean excitedly.

Sean thought for a minute. "Real light," he said. "It's made out of aluminum."

Brian jumped up, pushing back his chair. "Sean!" he said. "We've got the answer! Mr. Vanstedder stole the sketches and paintings. He knew that Mrs. Gomez would call the police, but it would take a while to work out the sale of the stolen art. He didn't want to take the chance that the police would search the employees' homes and find the stolen art there, so he hid the art inside the statue of Anubis in the museum."

Sean was confused. "OK, but what does his cane have to do with it?"

"It's probably hollow. Mr. Vanstedder lied about having an accident. He knew that everyone would get used to seeing him walk with a cane. If he took the art from the statue, rolled it tightly, and hid it inside the cane, he could walk right out of the museum with it."

Brian studied the photo again. "But you took a picture showing his cane far from his desk."

"Why would he care?" Sean asked. "I'm just a kid."

"Sure, you're a kid," he said, "but your

dad is investigating this case."

"Yeah!" Sean said. "And if Dad saw the photo of the cane so far from the desk, he'd figure things out. I bet that idea scared Mr. Vanstedder."

"Which means he'll probably try to get the stolen art out of the museum as soon as possible. Like tonight."

"How's he going to do it?"

"I'm not sure exactly," Brian answered. "But however he plans to do it, he'll have only a few minutes between the time the museum closes and when Mr. Potts begins to make his nightly check of the rooms. We need to get to the museum *before* it closes so we can stop him!"

CHAPTER NINE

Fifteen minutes before closing time, Brian and Sean slipped inside the museum in the middle of a noisy family group and followed it into the nearest art gallery.

"I thought we were going to the Egyptian room," Sean mumbled.

"We are, but not right now." Brian smiled. "I don't think Mr. Potts noticed us, so that means when the museum closes he won't come looking for us."

Sean shuddered. "You're kidding, aren't you? We aren't going to be here in the dark."

"It won't be completely dark," Brian said. "Haven't you ever noticed that the museum keeps dim night-lights on? Besides, you don't really believe Sam's story about the statue, do you?"

"Mr. Marshall said it was true."

"He did not," Brian said. "He said only that he knew about the legend."

"But what if the statue *does* walk?" Sean said. "We'll be trapped in here all alone with it."

"Would you quit worrying about the dumb statue," Brian said.

"Can't we just tell Mrs. Gomez what we suspect?" Sean asked.

"Mr. Vanstedder could just deny it," Brian said. "We won't have proof of what he's going to do until he does it."

"I don't know," Sean said.

"We've practically got this case solved," Brian said impatiently. "Do you want to help or don't you?"

"OK, OK," Sean said.

Studying the paintings and trying not to look suspicious, Brian and Sean slowly worked their way to the next-to-last gallery, ducked out the door, and entered the darkened lecture hall.

After they had been waiting a few minutes, a bell rang.

"The bell means the museum is closing," Brian told Sean. "There'll be an announcement over the public-address system next. It will be a while before George Potts makes his rounds and clears everyone out."

"What am I supposed to do until then?" Sean asked. He didn't enjoy hiding out in the dark.

"I don't know," said Brian. "Why not try dreaming about your girlfriend, Debbie Jean Parker," he teased.

"She's not my girlfriend!" hissed Sean.

"Sssh," said Brian suddenly. "I heard something."

Brian cracked the door open an inch and heard Mrs. Gomez. "George, after you've locked the doors and made your rounds, will you please join us in my office?"

"Just give me fifteen minutes," George called back.

"So far so good," Brian said. "Let's go to the Egyptian room, hide under the mummy case, and wait for Mr. Vanstedder to show up."

Sean and Brian crept silently into the Egyptian room. The dim overhead night-lights cast eerie shadows, and Sean shivered.

"This is giving me the creeps," Sean said.

"Be quiet," Brian said.

As they crawled under the mummy case, Brian grabbed Sean's arm and pointed. On the floor, within easy reach, was Mr. Vanstedder's cane. The handle had been removed, and they could see tightly rolled paper inside the cane.

"He got here before we did," Brian whispered. He looked toward the statue, but it was too dark to see anything. He reached out, grabbed the cane and its curved handle, and slid them under the case.

"Come on," Brian whispered to Sean as he fastened the handle onto the rest of the cane. "Let's get out of here." He began to inch backward.

Suddenly the statue lifted into the air and dropped onto its stand with a frightening *clang*. From under the mummy case, Brian and Sean saw a pair of hands fumbling along the floor.

"Run!" Brian whispered as he and Sean scrambled to their feet.

But before Sean could get away, a strong hand clamped down tightly on his shoulder.

"Give me that cane!" roared Mr. Vanstedder.

Brian stopped.

"Run, Brian!" shouted Sean. Suddenly, out of the corner of his eye, Sean saw a flash of gleaming metal. It was Anubis! And it was reaching out to grab him! Sean twisted out from Mr. Vanstedder's grasp and rolled out of the way just as the statue came crashing down.

"Arrrgh!"

Mr. Vanstedder threw up his hands, but the statue knocked him to the ground.

Sean was too frightened to move but not too frightened to yell at the top of his lungs.

The museum's main lights flashed on,

and George Potts appeared. Behind him came Mrs. Gomez, Ms. Brown, and John Quinn.

"Dad!" Sean shouted with relief. "We didn't know you were having your meeting here!"

Mr. Quinn and Mr. Potts lifted the statue from the floor, then helped Mr. Vanstedder to his feet.

"Dad," said Brian, "Mr. Vanstedder hid the paintings and sketches inside the statue. He put them into his hollow cane and was going to take them out of the museum."

"Ridiculous!" Mr. Vanstedder said. "This is all a mistake."

"A big mistake on your part," Mr. Quinn told him. He turned to Mrs. Gomez. "Call the police, Maggie. Mr. Potts can keep Mr. Vanstedder in custody until they arrive."

Mr. Quinn put his arms around Brian's and Sean's shoulders.

"That was good detective work," he said, "but you shouldn't have tried to handle it alone. I found out that Vanstedder had lied about visiting his doctor, and his telephone calls had been made to an Italian art collector who has been suspected of dealing in stolen art. I was ready to confront Vanstedder with the evidence."

"I'm sorry, Dad, but we had to act fast," Brian said. "Mr. Vanstedder blew it when he left his cane by the door and Sean got a picture of it. We knew he'd be in a hurry to move the art before Sean—or you, or anybody else—figured things out, and we had to be ready for him."

"You could have been hurt," Mr. Quinn told the boys. "If it weren't for Brian's being able to push that statue over onto Mr. Vanstedder . . . "

Brian interrupted. "I didn't push the statue, Dad. I was over near the door."

Mr. Quinn looked at Sean. "Well then, Sean, you must have pushed it over."

"It wasn't me," Sean said, shaking his head. He looked at Brian, who was staring at the statue with wide eyes.

"The only way the statue could have got this far from its stand," Brian said, gulping, "is if it walked!"

"It's impossible," Mr. Quinn said, puzzled. "It was probably just off balance and fell. After all, there *has* to be a logical answer."

"Sure, Dad," said Sean. "Whatever you say." But Sean knew what he had seen. Sam Miyako was right! The statue really had walked!

Sean walked over and playfully punched his brother in the shoulder. Now he was thinking about Sam's story about alligators in the sewers.

"I guess you won't be taking any baths for a while either, huh, Brian?"

Both boys burst out laughing.

Need a clue where to find exciting adventure?
Look for all the **Casebusters** books.

Here's an excerpt from *The Legend of Deadman's Mine . . .*

Brian pulled away the branches from the ledge and discovered an old wooden door cut into the rock.

"I knew it!" he said. "It's the entrance to Deadman's Mine! It's real!"

Brian grabbed hold of the old rusty handle and pulled as hard as he could. The door groaned as it slowly swung open.

"L-look!" shouted Sean. "It's th-the p-prospector's skeleton!"